IT CURD BE MURDER

RAISED AND GLAZED COZY MYSTERIES, BOOK 42

EMMA AINSLEY

SUMMER PRESCOTT BOOKS PUBLISHING

Copyright 2024 Summer Prescott Books

All Rights Reserved. No part of this publication nor any of the information herein may be quoted from, nor reproduced, in any form, including but not limited to: printing, scanning, photocopying, or any other printed, digital, or audio formats, without prior express written consent of the copyright holder.

**This book is a work of fiction. Any similarities to persons, living or dead, places of business, or situations past or present, is completely unintentional.

CHAPTER ONE

"I think you've lost your mind," Orson Hawley said as he sat on top of his stool in the kitchen of the Dogwood Donuts.

"Who?" Naomi Gardner, a longtime employee of the donut shop, asked.

"Maggie," Orson said decidedly.

"What makes you say such a thing?" Maggie Mission asked as she carried a large tray of dough to the baker's table.

"Because I've seen you work with that same dough three different times this morning," Orson said, shaking his head. "And here I thought I was the one in danger of age-related senility. I'm smack dab in the middle of old age, but what about you?"

"Orson, you should know better than to discuss a woman's age," Ruby Cobb said from the prep table next to the sink. As Maggie's business partner and best friend, Ruby spoke up in her defense.

"I haven't lost my mind," Maggie said at last. She concentrated on pressing softened butter into the dough.

"Then why have you been working with that same dough for the past several hours?" Orson asked.

"Because," Maggie said, looking up from the tabletop. "This is how you make authentic croissant dough."

"Why are you making croissants?" Orson asked.

"I'm not," she said matter-of-factly.

Orson huffed and shook his head. "You've got to be kidding me."

"She's making cronuts," Ruby answered for Maggie.

"And what on earth is a cronut?" Orson asked. He folded his arms defiantly over his chest and narrowed his gaze at Ruby. "That sounds like some sort of zombie hybrid donut."

"I guess that's one way to describe it." Maggie shrugged. She left the dough resting on the table for a moment and returned to the cooler.

"Now what are you after?" Orson grumbled.

"I made a raspberry glaze first thing this morning," Maggie said. She clutched a metal pan to her chest as she walked.

"Raspberry glaze?" Orson questioned. "Why not just use the glazing machine?"

"Because it's not actually a glaze," Ruby answered. As a trained executive chef and best-selling cookbook author, she often explained culinary mysteries in layman terms. "It's actually more of a thickened buttercream flavored with raspberry curd."

"I'm so confused," Orson said, tossing his hands up in the air.

"I'll tell you what," Maggie said. "You just wait around here for another hour or two and see what you think when these are finished."

"I still don't know what these even are," Orson shouted.

"Raspberry curd cronuts," Maggie said. "Haven't you been listening?"

"I see you rolling those out like a donut," Orson said. "And now I see you spreading that sauce or whatever it is in between the layers of the donut. I still don't know what you're making even when you say the words."

"Wait until you see what she does with the donut holes." Ruby chuckled. "Your mind will be blown."

"Hey, Maggie," Myra Sawyer Macklin said, entering through the swinging door from the dining area of the restaurant. "Oh, what are those?"

"Raspberry curd cronuts." Maggie smiled.

"That's right," Myra said, wagging her finger in the air. "This is what you were talking about last week. I can't wait to try one."

"You knew about this?" Orson snapped, directing his comment to Myra. "No wonder moving to a tropical location sounds so nice. If I'm there, I won't worry so much about these crazy notions you girls have."

"Sure, I knew." Myra raised a brow at him.

"You could have told me about it. After all, we do live under the same roof."

"When was I supposed to tell you?" Myra asked. "Between work, Brooks, and Lexi, when do I have time?"

"It isn't my fault your husband is the chief of police," Orson muttered. "I deserve to know what's going on around here. Especially when zombies are involved."

"Okay, everyone," Maggie said. "Just so there's no confusion, a cronut is a cross between a croissant and a donut. Ruby inspired this idea by her recent trip to France. She is the one who helped me with the raspberry curd sauce. And for the record, I will be injecting the sauce in the middle of the donut holes when they are finished."

"What is happening to this place?" Orson said, dramatically placing his hand on his forehead. "It's like I woke up this morning to a French bakery instead of a donut shop located in the middle of the Ozarks."

"I think that's a little excessive, even for you, Orson." Naomi stood watch over the automatic donut machines in the back of the kitchen as she spoke.

"What do you know about it?" Orson asked. "All you do is watch those machines make donuts for you."

"Oh, Maggie," Myra said, shaking her head. "I came back here for a reason. There's a man out front asking about Brett."

"That's strange," Maggie said. "I wonder what he wants."

"I'm not sure, but you might want to come out here and talk to him."

"Do you want me to come with you?" Ruby asked her.

"Yeah, maybe you should." Maggie wiped the flour from her hands on a towel and untied her soiled apron, placing them both on the table.

Brett Mission, Maggie's husband of several years, was also the former sheriff of Dogwood Mountain County, Missouri. While he spent his days running the smaller Jefferson Street location of the donut shop, his former career meant that old acquaintances sometimes had nefarious purposes for looking him up.

"Let's go then." Ruby followed Maggie through the swinging door, and they stood together behind the counter.

"Are you Brett's wife?" An older man approached her. Maggie was immediately uncomfortable by his proximity to the counter.

"First of all, do you mind stepping back from here?" she asked. "This area is for employees only."

"And what did you say your name is?" Ruby chimed in.

"I didn't," the man said. He removed his baseball cap and revealed a bald head. He narrowed his brown eyes at Maggie. "Which one of you is Brett's wife?"

"I am," Maggie said boldly. "Once again, please tell me your name."

"It's Andrew Finley.

"I'm sorry, but I'm not familiar with that name. Who are you to my husband, exactly?"

Stone faced; Andrew looked between the women. "I'm a retired law enforcement consultant from Hearth County. I've worked with Brett on a few things in the past."

"Oh," Maggie said, nodding. "You'll have to forgive me. Since Brett retired, it's a little concerning when someone shows up and wants to speak with him. You never know who might be looking for him."

"Or which side of the law they're from," Ruby added.

"Is that why you brought your bodyguard out here to meet with me?" Andrew asked, nodding in Ruby's direction.

"I'm not her bodyguard," Ruby said, perceivably offended. "But I am her best friend and business partner."

"Sorry about that," Andrew said. "I was just in town and thought I would look up an old friend. I didn't mean to cause alarm."

"But as someone in your position, I'm sure you understand our apprehension," Maggie said.

"Of course I do," Andrew said. He replaced the ball cap on his head and smiled for the first time. "In fact, I'll tell you what. If you direct me to a local hotel, then you can tell Brett where I'm at. That way the ball is in his court to contact me. Will that work?"

"Absolutely," Maggie agreed. "And I can do you one better than a local hotel. There is a large mansion on a hill overlooking the town of Dogwood Mountain that now serves as a bed and breakfast. It's called the Dogwood House, and I'll contact the owner, Gretchen, who is also a good friend, and see if she has any space available."

"A bed and breakfast," Andrew said. "That sounds pretty fancy."

"It's a really nice place," Ruby said.

"You both sound quite familiar with it."

"I am very familiar with it," Maggie informed him. "The house once belonged to my great-aunt, Marjorie, who also left me this business and my home. I grew up running around the Dogwood House. It's a beautiful piece of property and you will find it quite comfortable."

"Well then," Andrew said. "Why don't you make that phone call to the bed and breakfast, and then let your husband know he can find me there. We have quite a bit of catching up to do."

"How long have you been retired?" Ruby asked Andrew as Maggie stepped away to place her phone call.

"Just under two years now," Andrew said. "I tried my hand at a few part-time jobs before I decided the only occupation in my retirement future is fly fishing. That's why I'm down here."

"You've come to a good place," Ruby said, nodding. "We have quite a few rivers and streams in this part of the country."

"Yes, I know," Andrew said, smiling again. "I first became acquainted with this part of the state about eighteen years ago when Brett and I worked on a case together."

"Gretchen said to come right over," Maggie said, returning to the conversation. "She has a room ready for you. In fact, she only has one other guest booked this week."

"You're in for a treat then," Ruby said. "Gretchen will fuss over you like you've never been fussed over before."

"I like that idea," Andrew said. "Being single and older is not fun sometimes. A little attention goes a long way."

"You're single?" Maggie asked.

Andrew nodded slowly. "Another casualty of my career choice, I'm afraid." He eyed Ruby for a moment. "Forgive my boldness, but I don't suppose you're single?"

Ruby blushed immediately. "I am."

"Maybe we could have dinner while I'm here."

"Maybe we could all have dinner together," Ruby countered. She smiled nervously in Maggie's direction.

"That sounds like a plan," Maggie said. "But first, I'll let Brett know you're in town. He might be able to break away from work a little early and come and see you."

"Thank you." Andrew turned and headed toward the front door. "And thank your staff for not carrying me out of here on a pole."

"My staff?" Maggie asked. "Why would they run you out of here?"

"I don't know." Andrew shrugged. "But there are three of them standing behind that door there listening to every word we say."

"How do you know that?" Ruby asked, turning toward the swinging door.

"Because. I can see three distinct shadows in the space below the door. They have been standing there listening to our conversation. Believe me, I didn't spend over thirty years in my line of work without learning a few things." He touched the bill of his ball cap in their direction and headed out the front door.

CHAPTER TWO

"I don't remember this place," Andrew said as they sat down to eat at the steakhouse outside of Hunter Springs that Brett had suggested.

"That's because it wasn't here eighteen years ago," Brett said. He held Maggie's chair as she took her seat.

"Thank you, sweetheart," Maggie said.

"Look at you," Andrew said, shaking his head. "I remember you on several surveillance trips telling me you would never remarry."

"That was then," Brett said, grinning widely. "This is now."

"Tell me how you two met," Andrew said.

"We knew each other in high school," Maggie said. "Then I returned to town after moving away for several years."

"It's that simple?" Andrew asked. "You knew each other in high school and then you met again?"

"It's not quite that simple," Ruby said.

"She had a crush on me in high school." Brett shrugged. "I felt sorry for her when she came back to Dogwood Mountain."

"You're really pressing your luck tonight," Maggie said. She tossed her napkin in Brett's direction just as a server approached the table to take their order.

Maggie covered her face with her hands and laughed. By the time it was her turn to place her order, she had recovered slightly.

Andrew continued to watch the two of them. "Honestly, man. It's good to see you like this. The job can really get you down, you know."

"What happened to your relationship?" Brett asked. "Weren't you married?"

"I was." Andrew stirred his sweet tea without looking up. "That was another casualty of my job."

That's too bad," Maggie said.

"What about you, Ruby?" Andrew asked, turning his attention to his date. "Ever been married?"

"I never have been." Ruby smiled.

"Do you ever plan to be?" Andrew asked.

"Wow, that's a little forward," Brett said with a low whistle.

"At this stage in my life, no," she said bluntly. "I have the donut shop, my farm, my writing career. Life is pretty full as it is."

"Ahh, a writer you say? I've been known to dabble myself." Andrew nodded. "I can appreciate your answer, Ruby. I think you get to a certain age, and you realize it's not worth it anymore."

"Hang on a minute," Maggie protested. "Brett and I were past forty when we got married."

"Then you and Brett are an exception," Andrew said.

"I'm curious, Finley," Brett said. "What brings you back to this part of the state?"

"I was wondering when you'd get around to that question," Andrew said.

"Maybe he just wanted to look you up." Maggie elbowed her husband.

"There is that part," Andrew admitted. "But I also wondered what you remembered about the case that brought me here in the first place."

"You mean the blackmail letters?" Brett said.

"Oh, tell us more." Maggie raised a brow.

"Well, let's see," Brett said. "I think it began up your way, isn't that right, Andrew?"

"Hearth County is just south of the Iowa border, if you didn't know," he began, looking between Maggie and Ruby. "It seems odd that a case would tie together one of the northernmost and one of the southernmost counties in this state, but we had a couple of folks start receiving some threatening letters in the mail."

"What sort of letters?" Ruby asked, leaning forward in her seat.

Brett shook his head at her. "The letters demanded fifty thousand dollars from the victims, or they'd be turned over to the internal revenue service for tax crimes."

"What on earth?" Maggie said much too loudly. "What kind of tax crimes would even warrant something like that?"

"The usual." Andrew shrugged like it was the most normal thing in the world. "Tax evasion. Not reporting income correctly. Claiming nonprofit status when it wasn't correct."

"Right, and if I remember correctly, when a couple of the victims refused to pay up, they were run off the road," Brett said.

"Yeah, a couple were killed," Andrew said.

"That's terrible," Maggie said.

"How does all of this tie to Dogwood Mountain?" Ruby asked.

"It ties to both Dogwood Mountain and your neighbor, Jasper County," Andrew said. "A cousin of one of our victims up north received a similar letter here."

"And there was also a business owner in Hunter Springs who was killed outside of town," Brett said. "He received threatening letters, too."

"It sounds like the work of a serial killer." Ruby grimaced.

Andrew nodded slowly. "We were never able to establish that, but it does seem to fit the bill."

"When did it stop?" Maggie asked.

"That's just the thing," Andrew said. "We never did get a conviction. We had some suspects, but none that panned out."

"You seem to remember a lot about the case," Brett said. "I guess my memory is starting to fade a bit."

"Well, I've had to review the facts recently," Andrew said. He gazed in the distance.

"Something else is going on, isn't it?" Brett asked.

"You remember the Roland woman?"

"Alice, right?" Brett said, tilting his head.

"Yes. She ran a floral shop in my neck of the woods."

"I don't recall too much," Brett admitted. "She was run off the road, but she didn't die, right?"

"That's correct," Andrew said. "Anyway, the case seemed to go cold after her accident. The letters stopped rather abruptly."

"Look, buddy. I'm starting to get the feeling that you're about to say that the letters have started coming again," Brett said, staring him dead in the eyes.

Andrew nodded once and slowly sipped his sweet tea. He waited as the server placed their entrees on the table. "That's exactly what's going on," he said after the server left.

"Is that why you're here?" Maggie asked. "Do you think the case may become active down here as well?"

"I'm not sure," Andrew said. "I knew Brett retired, and I wanted to check in on things. I understand you're out of the loop these days, but I was hopeful you might remember something."

"No, he isn't," Maggie said. "He works with a group of retired law enforcement professionals looking into cold cases."

"Really?" Andrew leaned forward slightly, mimicking Ruby. "It sounds like you're taking a page out of my book as far as investigations go. Tell me more about this."

Brett eyed his wife. "We don't meet often, and we mainly have zoom meetings to review facts and cases. There isn't a lot of footwork involved."

"Have you had any success?" Andrew asked.

"Some." Brett smiled. "We've actually worked with a couple of innocent victim organizations and uncovered evidence that was missed."

"And you've also worked to overturn some wrongful convictions," Maggie pointed out.

"Have you really?" Andrew said. "That's unusual."

"We didn't start out that way, but following the evidence led us to different conclusions. We've had two successful overturns and subsequent charges filed against the actual perpetrator."

"Very impressive." Andrew clapped his hands and pointed at Brett.

"I know you didn't come here to review my track record. You need help, don't you?"

Andrew stared at his plate for a moment. "So far, I've only heard of one person getting a letter," he said when he looked up.

"Who might that be?" Brett asked.

"Me."

"You? You've been getting threatening letters?" Ruby squeaked.

"For the past two months," he said. "Only now they're coming more frequently. And the other night, I was out driving when a pickup nearly ran me off the road."

"Did you get a license plate number?" Maggie asked.

"Unfortunately, no," Andrew said. "The truck was moving too fast."

"Are you sure it was trying to run you off the road?" Brett asked. "Around these parts, we get plenty of young hot heads and their souped-up pickup trucks, who like to race around like no one's business."

"No, no." Andrew frowned. "He was absolutely trying to run me off the road, and I took it as a warning. The entire truck was tinted so dark I couldn't see the driver, despite how close he got to my tailgate."

"That's scary," Maggie said. "What did you do?"

"I went to my local sheriff, but they didn't want to listen to me. In fact, the sheriff told me she wasn't about to reopen a cold case based on nothing."

"Did you produce the letters?" Brett asked.

"I sure did," Andrew said. "I even pointed out that they had been written with a Germantown Rollerball."

"Is that significant?" Ruby asked.

"You can ask him," Andrew said, nodding in Brett's direction.

"The Germantown Rollerball is a unique pen," Brett explained. "We learned through the original case that the perpetrator was using a very specific type of pen to handwrite all of the letters."

"How can you be sure that's what this letter writer was using?" Maggie asked. "There are a billion different pens out there."

Andrew smiled. "Because in the past, we consulted a handwriting expert, and he showed us how to determine if the letter was written by that specific pen."

"You have to look at it very closely under a magnifying glass," Brett said. "Unlike other rollerball pens, the Germantown Rollerball has a wider top on the nib. So, the ink comes out looking a little flat."

"That is very specific," Ruby said.

Brett nodded. "It was very distinct. Our handwriting expert told us the writer probably used different angles of his or her hand to try to disguise the penmanship. But, they could prove it was written by the same person, specifically because of the signature of the rollerball."

"It sounds rather complicated to me," Maggie said.

"It is, and it isn't," Andrew said. "The writer attempted to make it seem as if there were multiple people sending the letters. But when our handwriting expert put the samples we provided under the microscope, he was able to determine the same person was writing them, just positioning their hands differently so it appeared as if it was multiple people."

"There was something about the pressure of the hand and the ink itself," Brett said. "I can't remember exactly why, but our expert told us that Germantown Rollerball pens were distinct in that way."

"Meaning it was difficult to disguise the handwriting?" Ruby asked.

"Yes," Andrew said. "It was impossible for the person to hide their own habits simply by changing hand positions."

"And even with that specific characteristic to the case," Brett said. "We were still never able to narrow down a conviction."

Andrew let out a heavy sigh. "There were multiple suspects, but the case has gone more than cold."

"I would say so," Ruby said. "If the sheriff of Hearth County is refusing to investigate it, that is."

"And that's why you're here," Maggie said. "You want Brett's help, right?"

"Why don't I take this to my cold case group? I can have them look over the facts and see if there's something we missed."

"I don't want someone else looking over this case," Andrew said, shaking his head. "That's not why I came."

"What could it hurt?" Brett asked. "My guys can take a look at these things and maybe they'll come up with something we missed. Who knows? Especially if you're being threatened. For all we know, it could be a copycat."

"Not a chance," Andrew said firmly. "This isn't a copycat. This is the original writer."

"That's a long gap in time," Maggie observed. "Maybe Brett's right and there is a copycat."

Andrew tossed his fork onto his plate. "Look, I'm not asking you for your help. I just wanted to know if you remembered anything about the case."

"I really don't remember a ton off the top of my head," Brett said. "I haven't even thought about this case in years."

"Then I guess my visit was a waste," Andrew said, standing suddenly. He nodded in Ruby's direction. "My apologies for ruining your evening."

"Andrew," Maggie called after him. "Don't leave."

"It was nice to meet you, Mrs. Mission," Andrew said as he walked toward the door.

"Brett, go after him," Maggie said.

"I'm going." Brett pushed back his chair and raced to follow his old friend.

"I wonder what that was all about," Ruby said while the two men spoke outside the restaurant.

"I'm not sure, but his mood sure changed quickly, and I didn't like it one bit."

CHAPTER THREE

"I'm going to bed," Brett announced as soon as he and Maggie walked through the back door of their house.

"You don't want to talk about what happened tonight?" she asked, following closely behind him.

"I didn't want to talk about it in the car, and I don't want to talk about it now."

"Brett," Maggie said. "This isn't like you."

"Yeah, well, even good guys have bad days." He walked down the hall and closed the bathroom door behind him.

Maggie rubbed the back of her neck and hung her coat on the hook near the back door before she began pacing around the kitchen.

"Everything okay?" Ruby texted her a short time later.

"No, actually," Maggie typed in reply. "Brett won't talk about it."

"Did he say anything on the way home?"

"Not a word," Maggie replied. "Aside from telling me that he didn't want to talk about it."

"I wonder what was said outside."

"Same here."

"Maybe you should try talking to Andrew."

Maggie stifled a laugh. "I'm sure that will go over well."

"We have to make our regular delivery to the Dogwood House in the morning. You could be the one to do that."

"What about the cronuts?"

"We'll get it done," Ruby assured her.

Maggie thought about it for a moment. Ruby's idea was a good one, even if it would annoy Brett. She finally agreed to make the delivery herself and then placed her phone on the charging cord as Brett left the bathroom.

"I'm headed to bed," he announced.

"Do you want company?" Maggie asked.

"Don't be that way," he called from the bedroom. "I just want to go to sleep. I don't want to talk about it anymore."

Maggie said nothing as she headed down the hall to the bathroom.

The following morning, Maggie carefully avoided the topic of conversation from the night before. Brett, still somewhat sour, drained a cup of coffee before heading out the door to the Jefferson Street location. Maggie had remained mum about her plans to deliver breakfast to the Dogwood House.

"Good morning," Myra said when she arrived at work. "How was dinner last night?"

"Eventful," Ruby said. "Don't ask."

"Seriously," Myra said. "What's going on?"

"Brett's old friend was in town to discuss a cold case," Maggie explained. "Only, this case is still very hot. When Brett suggested turning it over to his cold case group, Andrew got mad and left dinner."

"That seems weird. Why would he do that?" Naomi asked.

"Your guess is as good as mine." Maggie shrugged. She assembled a variety of pastries in a paper box.

"Are you making the run this morning?" Myra asked, eyeing Maggie as she worked.

"If that's okay with you," Maggie said.

"You're the boss," Myra said. "I'm just surprised."

"I'm not," Naomi said. "I bet the guy she was just talking about is staying there, isn't he?"

"He might be." Maggie smiled.

"You're going to ask him some questions, aren't you?" Myra chuckled.

"I thought I would check in on him," Maggie said. "I think that's a fairly reasonable follow up to what happened last night."

"It is," Ruby agreed. "And a good opportunity to find out more about this case."

"What makes this case so important all of a sudden?" Naomi asked.

"Like I said, it's suddenly very hot again. Apparently, the case involves blackmailed victims and threatening letters."

"And Andrew Finley, a consultant who worked on the case previously, has just begun receiving those letters himself," Ruby finished.

"Did he come to find out if Brett had received them as well?" Naomi asked.

"He didn't say that, but it makes sense," Ruby said. "Maybe that's why he got upset when Brett suggested the cold case group. He wasn't here for help, he just wanted to know if Brett had been threatened as well."

"And when he said he hadn't been, Andrew took it personally," Maggie said, understanding.

"How could someone take that personally?" Myra asked. "That's like getting offended that someone didn't shoot you, too."

"Or wondering why you were targeted and not someone else," Ruby added.

"That's a good point," Maggie said. "And that may be where I start my questions."

"You better get over there," Ruby said. "Gretchen will be calling us soon if we aren't there in the next fifteen minutes."

"You're right," Maggie said. She scooped up the boxes of donuts and other items then headed for the door.

Maggie carefully placed the boxes on the front seat and then returned to the kitchen for two drink trays filled with various lattes. Despite the fact that there were only two guests at the Dogwood House, she was determined to show up with various coffee choices. The lattes and coffees would not go to waste. Gretchen herself and her handyman, Albert, would avail themselves to the drinks if no one else consumed them.

"Good morning," Maggie said when she walked through the familiar back door that led to the kitchen of the bed and breakfast. Gretchen was seated at the large center island sipping a cup of coffee.

"Orson didn't mention you'd be the one coming today." Gretchen smiled. "Is Myra out sick?"

"No, nothing like that," Maggie said. "I just had dinner with your guest last night and thought I would say hello this morning."

"Oh, that's too bad," Gretchen said.

"Why do you say that?" Maggie asked. "Is he up yet?"

"Mr. Finley left in the middle of the night without even saying goodbye."

"You're kidding." Maggie set the boxes of donuts down on the counter. "He's gone?"

Gretchen nodded. "I'm afraid so. He left without paying his bill, too."

"I'll make it right with the bill." Maggie groaned, ready to go back out to the car for her purse.

"No, don't worry about that. He barely made a wrinkle in the bed. I'm tempted not to even strip it."

"Did he leave anything behind?" Maggie asked.

"I don't think so, but the way he left the room hardly demands a white glove inspection."

"He wasn't even here a full day. Why would he leave so fast?"

"Your guess is as good as mine," Gretchen said. "I wouldn't have even known he was gone if my other guest hadn't pointed it out to me this morning."

"Did you hear him leave?"

"Neither of us did," Gretchen said. "He was very quiet."

"How did your other guest know?" Maggie asked.

Gretchen offered an awkward smile. "The man wasn't here for long, but he somehow managed to make Miss Archer sweet on him. She went to his room this morning, claiming he'd promised to take her for a breakfast date, but there was no sign of him. She's rather upset about it."

Maggie shook her head. Andrew did seem rather curious about Ruby's relationship status, so it didn't surprise her that he had quickly moved on to getting attention from another woman.

"Speaking of being upset, I think Brett will feel the same way. They were talking about a case they both worked on almost twenty years ago, and then he just takes off."

"I sure wish there was something I could do to help," Gretchen said, reaching for a donut.

"It's not your fault." Maggie patted the older woman's arm. "But if you hear from him, please let me know."

The moment she was back in her car, she called Brett. After not getting an answer, she called him two more times with no luck. She left him a quick voicemail informing him of Andrew's abrupt departure just as she pulled back into the alley behind the donut shop.

After a brief explanation to Ruby and the others, Maggie dove into her work. She resumed her place at the baker's table and began assembling the croissant dough for the cronuts the following morning.

"You know you already have a dozen in the display case," Myra pointed out when she noticed Maggie bring out the cinnamon roll dough.

"I know," Maggie said. She stopped long enough to brush her hair off of her face with the crook of her elbow. "I just need to stay busy."

"You might want to stop for a moment," Orson said.

"Why would I stop?"

"Because Brett just pulled up out back," Orson said, quietly sipping his coffee.

"Brett's here?" Ruby asked. "How can you tell?"

"Because I know what his truck sounds like," Orson said. A second later, the back door opened, and Brett appeared before them. "See?"

"See what?" Brett asked.

"Never mind." Maggie sighed. "What are you doing here? I didn't expect to see you for another couple hours."

"Can we talk?" Brett asked, gesturing toward the back door.

"You want to talk outside?"

"If you don't mind," Brett said. His face was drawn.

"Okay, sure." Maggie stepped away from the baker's table and followed him through the back door. "What's going on?"

"Where were you when you left me that message?" Brett asked.

"Right here," Maggie said, indicating her parked car. "I called you before I went back inside. What's the matter? You're scaring me a little bit."

"Did you see or hear anything strange when you were driving back here from the bed and breakfast?"

"No, I didn't see anything unusual," Maggie said. "Why are you avoiding my question?"

"I don't mean to." Brett dropped his head and shrugged. "I just got a very concerning phone call from a deputy in Jasper County."

"Why would they be calling you?" Maggie asked, suddenly sick to her stomach.

"Because Andrew was run off the road last night. Witnesses saw him plummeting into the river right before the Highway 84 bridge."

"My gosh," Maggie said, covering her mouth with her hands. "They saw him go into the river?"

Brett nodded slowly. "Divers are looking for him now. He was observed going in from the oncoming lane."

"Did anyone see who was chasing him?" Maggie asked. "Did they get a description of the vehicle that forced him off the road?"

"That's just it," Brett said. "According to the deputy, Andrew had placed a 911 call in Jasper County just before he went off the road. He claimed he was being followed."

"But no one saw another vehicle?" Maggie said. "That's not good news."

"That isn't the only bad news. Andrew told the dispatcher if something happened to him, they needed to track me down to find out what was going on."

"He implicated you?" Maggie asked, dumbfounded by Brett's words.

"I'm not so sure if that's the way he meant it, but I get the feeling that's the way the sheriff took it. I tried to explain what was going on with the cold case, but they didn't seem very receptive."

"So, Andrew was run off the road and possibly killed, and his last words pointed the finger at you."

"I'm afraid that appears to be what happened." Brett hung his head. "I have someone covering for me at work. Do you think you could do the same?"

Maggie dashed back into the shop, vaguely explaining to Ruby what was going on. Less than five minutes later, she was on her way back home. Although Brett insisted she not share anything with anyone, she was certain Ruby had picked up that something was more wrong than what she was letting on.

"I can't believe any of this," Maggie said when she walked through the back door. "This whole situation is insane."

"My thoughts exactly," Brett said wryly. "I just wonder what they're going to find in that river."

"What do you mean?" Maggie asked. "I thought you said witnesses saw his truck go in."

"I'm not talking about the truck," Brett said. "I wonder if Andrew wasn't alone when he went off the road."

"You think someone was with him?"

"I don't know what to think," Brett admitted. "I'm just grasping at straws to be honest."

"It doesn't make any sense," Maggie stated.

"I can tell you something else that doesn't make sense." Brett pulled the chair away from the kitchen table and dropped into it. "It doesn't make any sense why I wouldn't have just listened to Andrew last night instead of getting all worked up and pushing the idea of investigating it with my cold case buddies."

"Come on, sweetheart," Maggie said, joining him at the table. "There was nothing inappropriate about that response. That's what I thought he was doing here, too."

"You thought he was here to talk to me about my cold case buddies?"

"No, I thought he was here to ask for your help investigating this case. He's the one who sought you out, and he's also the one who was receiving the threatening letters."

"Trust me," Brett said. "That's the part I'll remember for the rest of my life. I hate that he was targeted, and I wasn't."

"First of all, I hate that you'd even think that way, but I'm sure he was the one getting the letters because the person has a connection to his neck of the woods and not yours."

"How did you come to that assumption?"

"Because it makes sense," Maggie said simply. "You said this case involved counties on different ends of the state, right? If the suspect was involved with some of the people down this way, it makes sense that they would have targeted you. Instead, they sent the letters to Andrew. That makes me think whoever was sending him the letters had ties to the victims up north."

"I suppose that's possible," Brett said.

"You should call your buddies, because sitting here dwelling on this isn't going to do you any good," Maggie said. "And it's not going to do Andrew any good, either. Get on a call and lay everything out. Maybe they'll see something you aren't."

"Have you forgotten that was the last thing Andrew wanted me to do with this case?" Brett snapped.

"But it's probably the first thing you should have done," Maggie shot back. "Besides, you seem concerned that they may look at you as a suspect in whatever this is."

"I'm very concerned about that, which is why contacting my cold case group is a bad idea."

"No, that's exactly why calling together your buddies is the best thing you can do," Maggie said. "Can you think of a better way to look not guilty than to involve a half dozen former investigators? That definitely doesn't sound like someone with something to hide to me."

Brett sat up a little straighter and looked at his wife for the first time in several minutes. "That's really a good point."

"Good." Maggie smiled. "Don't let the dust settle on you. Go contact your group."

"I'll think about it," Brett said as he stood up. "But either way, I think I should be the only one to look into things with this case. Do you understand what I mean?"

"Hey, I'm just here to support you," Maggie said. Despite the sting in his words, she promised herself she'd let it go.

"I'm not trying to be a jerk, but I think only one of us needs to be involved in this investigation."

"Sure, of course. I get it," Maggie said. She watched him turn and leave the kitchen. A second later, the office door closed behind him.

CHAPTER FOUR

"You have another visitor out front," Orson announced around seven the following morning. He walked slowly to his stool near the sink and sat down, cradling his coffee as he walked.

"Who is it?" Maggie asked, slightly afraid of knowing the answer. Her heart raced in her chest as she wiped her hands off on her apron. No word had come about Andrew's fate since the announcement of his pickup truck careening into the river.

"It's not him," Orson said. "I know that's what you mean."

"Do you want me to go with you?" Ruby asked.

"No, I'll go," Maggie said. "I just had hoped it was…"

"We know what you were hoping," Orson said quietly. "You want it to be that Andrew guy popping up again just as much as the rest of us do."

Maggie said nothing as she pushed her way through the swinging door. She was only moderately surprised when she spotted the well-dressed woman on the other side of the counter.

"I'm Maggie Mission," she announced.

"Carla Johnson," the woman said. She extended her hand. "Is there somewhere we can talk?"

"Sure," Maggie said. She walked toward the end of the counter and slid into the booth in the corner.

"I have to admit I'm rather interested in something," Carla said, joining her.

"What's that?"

"That you didn't ask me for identification." Carla pulled something out of her breast pocket and slapped it down on the table. "I'm with the FBI."

"I'm married to a retired law enforcement officer. Sometimes things aren't that big of a shock, I suppose."

"Then you know why I'm here."

"I have an idea what this is about, but I don't know specifically why you're here."

"I just need to ask you some questions," Carla said. "Do you have a few minutes?"

"I'm the owner," Maggie said. "I can make time."

"That's right." Carla nodded. "You, your husband, and your son own this chain of donut shops."

"Our son... Is there any news?" Maggie interrupted herself, not caring if the agent knew the details of their business or not.

"About what?" Carla asked, plainly confused.

"Andrew Finley," Maggie said. "The last thing we heard was that his truck went off the road and into the river. Is he okay?"

"Listen, due to several factors, this river hasn't been maintained like it should be. It's dense with vegetation and his body has not been recovered yet," Carla said. "If that's what you're asking."

"Not exactly," Maggie said, sitting back against the seat. "I was hoping there was some chance he might have made it out alive."

"Do you know the river where he went in?" Carla asked.

"Just before the Highway 84 bridge," Maggie said. "I do know it. Pretty well."

"Then you know the likelihood of anyone making it out of that current alive is pretty close to zero," Carla said.

"Yes." Maggie sighed. "That doesn't mean I can't hold out some hope."

"I understand your thought process, but I also understand reality. At this point, our guys are working hard, but it's not an easy task. We've reached out to another team to get assistance."

"And the reality is that you believe my husband had something to do with Andrew being run off the road," Maggie said. "Is that what you came here to say?"

"I wasn't going to put it quite that way," Carla said, tilting her head to the side. "But since you brought it up, where was he that night?"

"Do you mean after we left the steakhouse or in the middle of the night?"

"Start with the steakhouse. What happened there?"

"They were discussing a former case they both worked on," Maggie said. "I'm sure you know which one I'm referring to. Anyway, Andrew let it slip that he had been receiving some threatening letters after nearly two decades of the case going cold."

"He just said that out of the blue?" Carla asked.

"Not exactly that way, but he did ask if Brett remembered the case. When Andrew revealed that the case had become active again, Brett suggested taking it to his cold case group."

"Tell me about the group."

"Brett didn't tell you already?" Maggie asked.

"I'd prefer to hear about it from you," Carla said. "What can you tell me about these people?"

"Not much," Maggie said. "I don't know a whole lot about them other than most of them are retired law enforcement. I think there's about a half dozen of them, men and women. They worked on all different levels."

"How often do they meet?" Carla asked, shrugging. "Are they nearby? How did Brett get to know them? Tell me everything you can."

"They mainly meet online," Maggie said. "I'm not sure exactly when Brett became familiar with them. He was in law enforcement long before we married."

"And you're sure that's what he's doing when he meets with this group?"

"Of course I am," Maggie said. "I've overheard meetings and even met some of them before. And I happen to know that they've had some success in their cold case investigations."

"Then do you have any reason why Andrew Finley would have not agreed to taking this case to them?"

"I have absolutely no idea why," Maggie said. "That's part of the reason why I delivered coffee and donuts to the Dogwood House, the bed and breakfast Andrew was staying at."

"Tell me about that," Carla said. "That was yesterday morning, right?"

Maggie nodded. "That's when I found out Andrew had checked out in the middle of the night."

"And the woman who runs that bed and breakfast is your aunt?"

"Oh, no, no," Maggie said, shaking her head. "Gretchen LeClair has become a friend, but she isn't any relation to me. My aunt used to own that house. Marjorie Getz was her name, but she died several years ago."

"My mistake." Carla smiled. "And to your knowledge, Andrew Finley has not been in contact with your husband in many years. Is that right?"

"That's exactly right," Maggie said. "As a matter of fact, I had never even heard his name before he arrived here asking for Brett."

"Okay." Carla drummed the table with her fingers. "That should do it for now."

"Those are all the questions you had for me?"

"Did you want me to ask more questions?"

"No, but maybe you can answer some for me," Maggie said. "Why does my husband think he's going to be a suspect?"

"That's probably better addressed to him not me," Carla said.

"No, that's not good enough," Maggie said. "There are witnesses here who can tell you what Andrew Finley said the day he came in asking about Brett. You can ask any one of my employees or many of our regular customers, and they will tell you exactly what Andrew said."

"And why would you suggest I do that?"

"Because that would tell you that my husband, in Andrew's own words, hasn't been in touch with him in many years," Maggie said. "And beyond that, you can talk to his friends, our son, our son's friends, and many other people who will tell you that Brett is a law abiding, decent human being. They will also tell you that Brett was proud of his work with the cold case group."

"I don't doubt that he's proud of it," Carla said. "He said as much to me."

"Then why would he be a suspect?" Maggie asked. "Let's just address the elephant in the room. I know you can't tell me too much, but we both know there's a reason why you're here. So why would someone still dedicated to upholding and sustaining the law be on the wrong side of it?"

"You're right about one thing," the agent smiled awkwardly. "I can't... and won't, tell you too much. I'm here to ask the questions I see fit."

They chatted for a little while longer, and then the FBI agent made her way to the other side of the dining room. She turned around once and nodded in Maggie's direction before she headed out the door. Maggie felt her knees grow weak and sat back down hard in the booth. She rested her head in her hands, elbows propped up on the table, and shook her head side to side.

"Are you okay?" Ruby asked, approaching the booth.

"I don't know," Maggie whispered. "I don't know if I'm alright or not."

"I'm so sorry," Ruby said, sliding in across from Maggie. "I can't believe they would even consider that Brett had anything to do with this."

"You heard?" Maggie asked, looking up.

"I was standing right here the whole time," Ruby said, nodding to the end of the counter. "You didn't realize that?"

"Not really." Maggie shrugged. "My head is spinning. This is all so surreal. Brett being a suspect in this crime is beyond my wildest thoughts."

"It doesn't sound like there's actually a crime yet," Ruby said. "If the body hasn't been recovered."

"I don't know," Maggie argued. "It kinda sounds to me like they believe him to be dead, despite the lack of a body. I know it's not all final yet, and the outcome could be very different if Andrew is dead, but someone even thinking Brett could have chased someone down, ran them off the road, and sent them careening into the river is almost too much for me to handle."

"There has to be some sort of mistake," Ruby said. "They can't just assume the one person Finley spoke to about this case is the guilty party."

"It makes me wonder what else they know," Maggie said.

"Maybe this time Brett's friends can step in and solve a case for him."

"Maybe," Maggie said. "I hope someone steps in, and fast."

CHAPTER FIVE

"I'm not going to work tomorrow," Brett announced when Maggie came home.

"I don't blame you," she replied. "Do you have any plans?"

"Really? You're not upset?" Brett took a seat on the couch and looked up at her.

"Why would I be upset? Unless you plan to do something reckless or stupid, of course."

"Honestly, I planned a meeting with my cold case squad," he said. "It may take all day."

"Then you've decided to take Andrew's case to them?"

"I don't think I have any other choice. I've already involved them, anyway."

"You have?" Maggie raised a brow.

"I panicked a little bit after I found out Agent Johnson came to visit you, and I ended up reaching out to them." He rested his elbows on his knees and shook his head.

"What was their response?" Maggie asked. "I assume it was good, given the fact you want to go further into the case with them."

"One of my buddies is a former FBI agent himself. He gave me some pointers but did say he won't get directly involved. Everyone else was on board, so I sent them the information I had on the case and asked them to look over things."

"How worried are you?" Maggie asked.

"I was worried," Brett admitted. "Frankly, I worry about a lot of things, but I know where I've been and what I've done."

"But Brett, based on your work with the cold case group, you are very aware of the fact that sometimes

IT CURD BE MURDER

justice doesn't lead to the right conclusions. What if something goes wrong in this case?"

"I can't focus on that right now."

"We have to be realistic."

"Agent Johnson was fishing," Brett said. "She was looking for holes in my story. That's what most investigators do."

"And you're confident that she's not going to rush to judgment or take things the wrong way?"

"I'm not confident of anything," Brett said. "But, I have to do my best to figure out what's going on. Zeke is going to cover for me tomorrow."

"So, you already talked to Bradley?" Maggie asked, referring to her son and Zeke's boss at another one of their donut shop locations. Her heart ached at the thought of Brett approaching him with news of the investigation.

"I didn't have to," Brett said. "Agent Johnson had already visited him."

"She did what?" Maggie said, spinning into mama bear mode.

"She interviewed him right after she left you. She asked him about me and our relationship. She even asked why you called him 'our' son and not just your son."

"That's infuriating."

"Maggie, she's doing her job," Brett said.

"I wish she'd come back into the donut shop," Maggie said, ready to spit fire. "I have plenty I want to say to her now."

"And this is exactly why I'm going to look into this case," Brett said. "And I don't want you anywhere near it."

"You said that already," Maggie reminded him.

"I know, and I'm saying it again. I know you've been successful before, but this time just do me a favor, and stay away from it."

"That's not fair."

"Maybe not, but it's necessary. And I'm not going to discuss it further."

The discussion was over. Maggie and Brett said little more to each other before they went to bed, and even less before work the following morning.

When Brett retreated to the living room with a cup of coffee, Maggie headed to the donut shop, happy to get out of the house.

"Good morning," Ruby said when she walked into the kitchen.

"I hope so," Maggie said.

"That sounds ominous." Ruby laughed. "What's going on?"

"Just some tension at home."

"I'm not surprised," Ruby said. "Brett is under some scrutiny right now. Of course he's upset."

"He arranged with Zeke to take over the Jefferson Street location today. He plans to confer with his cold case group all day about the case."

"That's probably a good thing."

"I suppose, but he also made it plainly clear that he doesn't want me looking into things. In fact, he practically banned me from doing it."

"That doesn't sound like Brett. He's always telling you to be cautious but never straight up tells you no.

Which I'm sure makes you want to look into things even more." Ruby grinned.

"I guess it does," Maggie said. "I just feel so helpless."

"Give it a little while," Ruby encouraged. "Who knows? Brett may have a completely different outlook on things after talking to his group today. You know how effective they can be."

"I know you're right, but I found out that the agent talked to Bradley yesterday. I don't know why, but that really got me upset. I feel like she's an unwelcome guest in my house."

"You feel violated."

"More or less," Maggie said.

"You know she just went there because she was hunting for something."

"That's basically what Brett said, only he called it fishing."

"Hunting, fishing, it's all the same thing," Ruby said. "My guess is she's just casting a wide net to see what she can catch."

"And I know that's her job, but it's disturbing to me. Andrew appeared here out of nowhere, and now my husband is somehow involved."

"Your husband simply has the attention of an FBI agent for the moment. Look at all the different aspects of this case. Remember the unique pen they mentioned? It won't take long for them to realize that Brett doesn't own one. It also won't take long for them to realize he has multiple witnesses who will attest to his whereabouts. They might go so far as to search your home, and they will find nothing. Absolutely zilch."

"Aside from the part about them searching my house, that was pretty comforting."

"Let's just get through the day," Ruby encouraged. "We'll sit around the fire tonight and enjoy a glass of wine and do our best to put this out of our minds. Does that sound good?"

"That sounds perfect."

CHAPTER SIX

"So how is everyone?" Dogwood Mountain Police Chief, Brooks Macklin, asked later that night. He was seated next to his wife, Myra, across the bonfire from Brett and Maggie.

"That's what I want to know," Orson asked. He stared directly at Brett. "How is everyone?"

"Don't look at me," Brett said. "I've had better days."

"Hey, man," Brooks said. "Myra filled me in a little bit on what's going on, and I've spoken to Agent Johnson myself. I just wanna let you know I'm aware of what you're going through."

"Really?" Brett scoffed. "You know what I'm going through? No offer to help?"

"Brett, calm down," Maggie said. "Brooks has to stay out of personal matters. You know better."

"You better start talking, young man," Orson said, wagging his finger in Brett's direction. "You blow up like that and you owe everyone an explanation."

"I'm sorry, but I don't have an explanation to give this time."

"That's not good enough," Orson said. "I've never seen you talk to your best friend that way."

"It's okay," Brooks said. "Brett's under a lot of pressure."

"What did I miss?" Ruby asked when she appeared at the edge of the circle of chairs. "I have brownies."

"What kind?" Naomi asked.

"Any kind you can imagine." Ruby handed the tray to Naomi and took her seat next to Maggie. Naomi passed the tray to Orson after she had made her selection.

"You missed Brett jumping down everyone's throat," Orson said, angrily staring at the brownies like they'd personally attacked him.

"That's not quite fair," Myra said.

"Tell me that isn't what I just saw," Orson said.

"Can we not do this right now?" Brett pleaded.

"Then when?" Orson asked. "You show up here with a chip on your shoulder. Anytime anyone asks you how you're doing, you jump at them. Tell me when a better time is to have this discussion?"

Brett stood up suddenly and threw his arms over his head. "An FBI agent visited my wife and my son asking about me. An old acquaintance showed up out of the blue, and now I'm a suspect in whatever this is. And to add insult to injury, my group of cold case investigators suddenly won't touch this case with a ten foot pole."

"Your cold case group wouldn't look into things?" Ruby asked. "Did they give you a reason?"

"Conflict of interest," Brett said flatly. "That's the reason they gave me. There's a potential each of them might be questioned in turn and even though they all agreed to check things out, they changed their minds. Every last one of them."

"But have they been questioned?" Ruby asked gently.

"Not yet, but that doesn't mean anything."

"Surely this agent has more to focus on than just you," Brooks said.

"You wouldn't know it by her actions," Brett grumbled.

"I don't think that's true," Maggie said. "No one here has been questioned, aside from the two of us."

"That is a good point," Brooks said. "We both know that's a good sign."

"Yeah, maybe," Brett said. "Look, I'm going to walk around for a bit. Is that okay, Ruby?"

"Of course," Ruby said, sweeping her hand around the large field surrounding them. "You know you're welcome. Just take a brownie with you when you go."

Brett nodded solemnly. He picked a brownie up from the tray and headed toward the gravel driveway. Maggie watched him disappear into the darkness.

"He's really upset, isn't he?" Myra asked when Brett was out of earshot.

"He is," Maggie said, nodding. "I've never seen him like this before."

"Probably because this is a pretty unique situation," Brooks said. "I'm not surprised he's upset."

"Neither am I," Maggie said. "But he won't let me help him."

"In what way?" Brooks asked. "Do you mean personally looking into things?"

"He essentially forbade me," Maggie said.

"Wow," Brooks said. "That's pretty heavy, but maybe he just wants to keep you safe."

"I feel like my hands are tied." Maggie hung her head.

"Can't you just do it anyway?" Naomi asked.

"Says the woman who is single," Orson said.

"Are you telling me you don't think Maggie ought to look into this case?" Naomi challenged him.

"I never said that. I'm just saying it's more complicated when you're married. People tend to have their thoughts clouded when love or romance are involved."

"What if I look into things?" Ruby asked. "If I'm the one who takes the lead and investigates, Brett can't say much."

"Okay," Myra said. "Where do we start?"

"I'd like to be included," Naomi added.

"Great, now we have Charlie's Angels on the case." Orson frowned.

"Don't you mean Orson's Angels?" Brooks said.

"This is getting out of hand," Maggie said. "I'll look into things too, but the rest of you don't need to worry about it. If Brett gets mad at me, I will deal with him."

"We'll all do it, and if Brett gets mad at the rest of us, he can just get over it," Ruby said. "We are his friends, after all."

"Orson, what do you say the two of us go inside and find a refill for our wine glasses?" Brooks suggested, standing up.

"You want to leave?" Orson said.

"He sort of has to," Myra said. "He's still a cop, remember?"

"Fine, but why do I have to go?"

"Because this is a girl's only club." Ruby winked.

"Fine, fine," Orson said. He stood slowly and followed Brooks toward the house.

"Now that they're gone," Ruby said. "Where do we start, Maggie? What do you know about this case?"

"Are you guys serious about this?" Maggie asked.

"I'm serious," Naomi said.

"So am I," Myra said. "We don't have much time before the guys come back."

"Myra's right," Ruby said. "Give us the skinny on the case while they're gone."

"Well, Andrew first contacted Brett about eighteen years ago. He was working on a case up north in Hearth County involving blackmail letters."

"What was the threat?" Naomi asked.

"The letters threatened to turn people over to the IRS for tax crimes of various sorts," Maggie explained. "Unless they paid out fifty thousand dollars."

"How did that case relate to Dogwood Mountain County?" Myra asked.

"There were other threats sent to people down here," Maggie said. "And I guess one of the victims up north had a relative down here."

"How many witnesses are left now?" Naomi asked. "That's one of the first things we need to address."

"That's a good point," Ruby said, looking at Maggie. "I'm sure you've already done a little research, so tell us what you know so far."

"Well, Larry McVie still lives down this way," she said. "His cousin was a victim up north. I forget his first name, but he owned a tire shop."

"Myra, write that down," Ruby said. "Larry McVie."

"I don't have a pen and paper," Myra said.

"I'll make a note on my phone," Naomi said. "And then I'll share it with everyone else."

"Perfect, perfect," Ruby said. She clasped her hands together and pointed her index fingers at Maggie. "What else do you remember?"

"There was a man named Jackson Myers in Hunter Springs," Maggie said. "He had a small shipping company and was killed when he was run off the road."

"I think I remember something about that," Ruby said. "He went into the river, right?"

"I don't know for sure, but that's eerily familiar." Maggie frowned. "I guess I need to go over some notes myself."

"How many victims were there in total?" Myra asked.

"Honestly, I don't know," Maggie said. "I probably should look into that as well."

"Are there any other victims that lived down this way that you're aware of?" Ruby asked.

"There was someone over in Jasper County," Maggie said. "I think he was the reason Andrew knew to look down this way at first. He had homes here and up north. Anyway, he was an accountant and was killed in a similar accident."

"Anyone else?" Naomi said.

"Alice Roland," Maggie said. "They were talking about her the other night, Ruby. Remember?"

"Right, she was a florist or something, but I'm not sure I remember her ties to this area."

"I'm not sure there were any," Maggie admitted. "But I'll check it out and try to see where she lives now."

"I think we have decent a place to start," Naomi said eagerly. "Why don't you go home tonight and get as much information as you can together, and then we can talk about this in the kitchen tomorrow."

"But what about Orson?" Myra said. She glanced toward the farmhouse. "What if he tries to get involved?"

"We'll tell him we want him to wash the dishes," Ruby said. "You know how he reacts the moment we suggest he pitch in."

"He usually runs for the hills," Myra said.

"That's what I'm counting on." Ruby smiled.

CHAPTER SEVEN

Maggie hugged a stack of papers against her chest the following morning. With her free hand, she shoved her key into the back door and turned the lock. She was surprised when Ruby appeared on the other side of the door and held it open for her.

"I didn't see your truck," Maggie said. "I didn't know you were here already."

"Naomi picked me up," Ruby said. "My truck didn't want to start. I've got the mechanic working on it now."

"Naomi is here?" Maggie said. She looked around the kitchen.

"Myra and Naomi are already out front," Ruby said. "We all agreed to get here a little early today."

"Goodness." Maggie smiled. "Is everyone that eager to help out with this case?"

"More than eager," Ruby said. "You have no idea."

For the first time in what felt like forever, Maggie felt a bit of the burden of worry lift from her shoulders. She headed straight for the office where she deposited the paperwork on her desk, then turned back to the kitchen. She swiped a clean apron off the hook and tied it around her waist.

"What did you just put in the office?" Naomi asked, standing in front of the prep table.

"Some facts about the case," Maggie said. "I printed off everything I could find about it."

"What did Brett think you were doing?" Myra asked, appearing behind Naomi.

Maggie smiled broadly. "I told him we were going to try a different variety of donuts. I don't know if he bought it or not."

"Good move." Myra laughed. "Why don't you give us the rundown while we start our first batch for the display case."

"Let me get my supplies." Maggie headed for the storage room and returned with a container of flour, cinnamon, and yeast. She quickly assembled the dough for her cinnamon rolls. "I found out something interesting."

"We're all ears," Ruby said as she continued to shred apples for her apple slaw.

"Remember the accountant I mentioned who was killed in Jasper County? Well, he had an employee named Sarah Houston who was a suspect at one time," Maggie explained.

"Is Sarah still around?" Myra asked.

"No, but her twin sister Hannah is."

"Did you find an address?" Ruby asked.

"I sure did." Maggie grinned. "She lives in Jasper County."

"Then I think we ought to pay her a visit after work," Ruby suggested.

"Do you want all of us to go?" Naomi asked.

"You and Maggie should go," Myra said. "Naomi and I can go down to the Highway 84 bridge and try to take photos of the spot where Andrew went off the road. I don't know if they'll let us in the area, but I'm more than willing to try."

"Actually, I have a better idea," Ruby said. "I'll go with Maggie, but why don't we look over the paperwork Maggie brought in and see if there are any other leads we can follow up on."

"Isn't that what we're doing?" Maggie said.

"I mean, let's see if we can find any references to other cases in Hearth County," Ruby said. "Then Myra and Naomi can research those cases and find any other names in common between north and south. We don't have forever to investigate things. The most productive use of our time would be to find ties between the two areas, not worry about getting into trouble because we're hanging around a crime scene."

"Fair enough." Maggie laughed. "Are we all on the same page?"

After everyone agreed, they worked together for the remainder of the morning. Maggie felt her spirits rise as they chatted about the investigation. She discussed plans with Ruby during their morning break and was surprised when Myra appeared with a slip of paper and set it on the table between them.

"What's this?"

"An address for Larry McVie," Myra said, tapping it. This is thanks to Naomi. She apparently has a knack for that sort of thing."

Maggie looked at the paper. "This should be helpful. Let's get back to work, though, so we don't spend all our time thinking about the case."

Around two o'clock, Naomi suggested Ruby and Maggie take off for the day. They both agreed and disappeared into the employee bathroom to freshen up.

"Ready to go?" Maggie asked a few minutes later as she made her way to the back door.

"Ready as I'll ever be." Ruby entered the address into the GPS on her phone and they headed south to the outskirts of Dogwood Mountain. Ruby directed her street by street until they reached the house. "Here we are," Ruby announced.

"I'm not interested," the gravelly voice called through the front door as they walked up.

"We're not selling anything," Maggie announced.

"I don't need religion either."

"We're looking for Sarah Houston's sister," Ruby said. "Are you Hannah?"

"Who's asking?"

"My name is Maggie, and this is Ruby. We just had some questions for you about a case your sister was involved in."

"I have nothing to say about that," the woman said. She appeared behind a screen door for the first time. "That was a long time ago."

"Do you remember the letters?" Maggie asked. "They've started again."

"Oh, no," the woman said. She bowed her head sadly. "You've got to be kidding."

"We know your sister was a suspect," Ruby said. "Obviously, they were wrong since it's happening again."

"You have no idea how wrong they were," Hannah said, raising her head. Her words came sharp and quick. "They drove her to her grave, you know. Just because that boss of hers ran his truck off the road, doesn't mean she had a thing to do with it."

"Do you remember anything your sister might have told you about that time?" Ruby asked.

"I already told you she was innocent," Hannah snapped.

"I believe she was," Ruby said.

"Then what are you doing here?" Hannah asked.

"I just wanted to see if there was anything you might remember that could help us now," Ruby said.

"Why would I help you?" Hannah asked. "I've already told you my sister is gone. They can't do anything to her anymore."

"Ma'am," Maggie said curtly. "The blackmailer, whoever is behind these letters, has begun again. Andrew Finley, an investigator from up north in Hearth County who worked this case almost twenty years ago was just driven off the road into the river. He was the one receiving the threatening letters."

"I remember him," Hannah said. "He's dead?"

"Nothing is confirmed, but the last I heard, they haven't been able to pull his body from the river yet," Maggie said. "Andrew paid my husband a visit and revealed that the letters had been coming again. He was run off the road right after."

"I'm sorry," Hannah said. "But I can't help you. The only thing I have to say is, 'good riddance.'"

"Good riddance," Ruby repeated.

"You heard what I said. That man made my sister's life impossible. I'm not sorry he's gone." She stepped to the side and pushed the door shut.

Maggie heard the lock click. "I have to get her to talk."

"It's not going to do us any good," Ruby said calmly. "Hannah is clearly finished with this discussion."

"But she knows more," Maggie said. "I'm sure of it." She rapped three times on the door and waited.

"Let's go," Ruby said. "She's already said everything she is willing to say. We need to leave her alone."

"But if she knows something, maybe it will help take the attention off Brett."

"Agent Johnson will turn her attention somewhere else in due time," Ruby said. She stepped from the concrete porch and headed toward Maggie's car.

"We don't know that for sure." Maggie remained outside the door with her arm raised ready to knock again.

"We do know," Ruby said. "Because there's no evidence that links Brett to this case or to Andrew's wreck. Think about it, Maggie. This matter will take care of itself."

"If you didn't want to come with me, you should have said something." Maggie breezed past Ruby and headed for her car.

"I never said I didn't want to come with you. I'm just saying that this interview is a dead end. I want to figure out who's behind this as much as you do."

"Why?" Maggie said. "It isn't your husband dealing with all of this."

"Maggie," Ruby said sharply. "Not only was that uncalled for, but it wasn't fair. You know how much I love Brett and you. I want to find out who is behind this for many reasons."

She gripped the steering wheel and rested her forehead against it. "I don't know what just came over me. I'm sorry I spoke to you that way."

"I know what came over you," Ruby said. "You're under a lot of added pressure. That's bound to put anyone on edge."

"I know," Maggie said, turning toward her friend. "But that's no excuse to speak to you the way I just did. I'm truly sorry. You didn't have to go with me today, and I appreciate you being here."

"We're good," Ruby said. "Why don't we give the other two a call and see what they've come up with?"

"That sounds like a plan." Maggie said, grateful that her best friend was so understanding,

CHAPTER EIGHT

"We found something," Myra said over speakerphone a few minutes later. "We were looking through some of the paperwork that you brought in this morning. There's an address for a man named Malcolm Price, a former member of The Selectboard from a place called Auburn Grove."

"Auburn Grove? That's up north," Ruby said.

"Precisely," Myra said. "It's in Hearth County. Anyway, according to the notes, Andrew suspected Malcolm at one point."

"Do you know why?" Maggie asked.

"I assume it was because he had intimate knowledge of businesses in both counties."

"What was his connection to Dogwood Mountain?" Ruby asked. "Or even Jasper County, for that matter."

"We're still not sure, but the most interesting part of it is that he has an address listed in Dogwood Mountain."

"Was he ever ruled out as a suspect?"

"According to what we could find, yes," Myra said. "He had alibis that placed him out of the country when some of the notes were sent in the mail. He simply could not have sent them. Besides, it was later proven that he stood to lose if some of the businesses that were targeted failed."

"I'm really confused," Maggie said. "How would he stand to lose if a local tire shop failed?"

"The shop was located in his district," Myra explained. "If that shop went out of business under his stewardship, it wouldn't have benefitted him in any way, especially during the election that was coming up. His opponent didn't need more fuel added to the fire."

"What's the address?" Ruby asked. "We can run over there on our way back."

"Why don't we meet at your house in a couple of hours, Ruby?" Myra suggested after she read off the address. "We can compare notes without any interruptions."

"That works for me, but what is Maggie going to tell Brett?" Ruby asked.

"Nothing," she said. "Unless he asks. Anyway, this address is on the outskirts of town. We're headed there now."

"Be careful," Myra said. "Hey, how'd things go with Hannah?"

"It didn't pan out, but we'll explain more later," Ruby promised. "See you in a little while." She arranged her phone on the dashboard and pressed the button to begin navigation to their destination.

Maggie headed out on the highway and a half an hour later, they found themselves parked at a crossroads at the foot of the mountain just north of town.

"I don't see a road sign," Ruby said. "But according to my GPS, this has to be Sassafras Hollow Road."

"Are you sure your GPS is working?"

"Not entirely." Ruby chuckled. "But I do have full signal here. I think we should just trust it."

"As you wish." Maggie reluctantly headed down the unmarked road. After a half mile or so, the woods on either side of the road thinned out and houses appeared on either side. "These houses must be situated on ten acre lots."

"At least," Ruby said. "Look. There's a fancy mailbox with the address stamped on a metal sign. This is Sassafras Hollow Road."

"What was the house number again?"

"1205. I think that's it," Ruby said, pointing out the passenger window. "Just there at the top of the hill. That is a very large house."

"Yes, it is." Maggie pressed firmly on the brakes and turned her signal on, ready to pull into the long driveway. "Look at that sign in the yard. I don't think this is just a normal residence."

Ruby squinted. "What does it say?"

"The lettering is a little faded, but I think it says Sassafras Hollow Assisted Living."

"A nursing home?" Ruby gazed at the large structure as they eased slowly down the driveway. "This is a pretty fancy place."

"Looks like a parking lot in the back," Maggie said. "Yes, and there are more signs. This is definitely an assisted living facility."

"Do you think the girls made a mistake?"

"Not necessarily," Maggie said. "Malcolm Price could very well live in a place like this."

"But don't you think it's odd that he would live down here and not up north where he's from?"

"I guess we're about to find out." Maggie pulled into a narrow parking spot on the far edge of the gravel lot. Moments later, they approached the entrance of the building.

"Can I help you?" came the metallic voice through a small speaker on the right side of the door.

"Yes, we're here to visit a resident," Ruby said quickly.

"Name?"

"Malcolm Price," Ruby said.

"You can enter," the voice said. The lock clicked open, and Maggie reached for the doorknob.

"This place certainly smells like a nursing home," Ruby said as they entered. The lower level of the large house had been decorated much like a waiting room at the hospital. They followed the linoleum floor down a wide hall to a reception desk.

"You're here to see Malcolm Price?" A young man dressed in scrubs asked from behind the desk.

"That's right," Maggie said.

"Go down the hall, up the steps, his room is on the second level. Room 18," the orderly said without looking up from his phone.

"Do we need to sign in or anything?" Maggie asked, unsure why they weren't asking more questions or any at all, really.

"Nope," the orderly said.

"Come on." Ruby grabbed Maggie's arm and dragged her down the hall toward the stairwell.

"Why did you do that?"

"Because you were going to ask so many questions that young man might forget to be more interested in his phone and actually wonder what we're doing here."

"Good point," Maggie said. "What kind of assisted living facility doesn't have an elevator?"

"Another good point," Ruby said.

When they reached the top of the steps, they stepped out of a short hallway and into a large room. A row of recliners was set up in front of large floor to ceiling windows. The rest of the space was filled with tables and chairs, with a kitchen area to their immediate right.

"I guess we should go this way," Maggie said, pointing to her left.

"Lead the way," Ruby whispered. As they headed toward the hallway, several residents and workers dressed in scrubs nodded in their direction, but no one stopped to question their presence.

"He said Room 18 right?" Maggie asked as they entered the hallway.

"It looks like the numbers get bigger down the hall," Ruby observed.

The name Malcolm Price was written on an index card and shoved into a plastic frame next to the door at the end of the hallway. Maggie knocked lightly on the wooden door and waited.

"Come in," a woman's voice called through the door.

"We're looking for Malcolm Price," Ruby announced as she turned the doorknob.

"And who might you be?" asked a young woman with long, dark hair braided down her back. She sat on the arm of a recliner. An older man, dressed in a T-shirt and sweatpants, sat in the recliner with his feet propped up. His head was turned toward the window where he appeared to gaze out at the road in front of the large house.

"My name is Maggie Mission, and this is my friend and business partner, Ruby Cobb."

"Laura Price," the younger woman said. "I assume you're here to see my father, Malcolm."

"Yes, we are," Ruby said. "How is your dad doing?"

"About as well as you can see." Laura stood up from the side of the recliner and folded her arms. "Who are you and what do you want with my dad?"

"Was your father a member of the selectboard in Auburn Grove?" Maggie asked.

"Decades ago," Laura said. "What is this about?"

Maggie tried hard to soften her features. "Do you remember anything about a series of blackmail letters back then?"

"Of course I remember." Laura narrowed her eyes. "You better not be reporters. If you are, I'll toss you out that window myself."

"We are not reporters," Ruby said quickly. "As a matter of fact, we're just a couple of local business owners."

"Then why on earth are you here to talk to my dad about this? If you knew anything about it, you would know that's part of the reason why he's in the state he's in today."

"I'm afraid I don't understand," Maggie said.

"Do you have any idea how much stress and strain that case put on my dad?" Laura asked. "Even his doctors agree that that stress probably led to his cognitive demise. He barely speaks and I finally had to place him in a facility because I couldn't care for him in my home anymore."

"And your home is where?" Ruby asked.

"Not that it's any of your business, but I grew up outside of Hunter Springs. My dad and mom divorced when I was little, and she moved down south. My dad remained up north."

"And that's his tie to this area," Maggie whispered.

"I'm not going to ask you again," Laura said. "Who are you?"

"Do you remember the name Andrew Finley?" Maggie asked. "He was a consul…"

"Get out," Laura said suddenly.

"Pardon me?" Maggie stepped back.

"If you're here on behalf of that horrible man, you can just get out right now."

"We're not here on his behalf," Ruby explained. "But we are here because of him."

"Andrew Finley was recently run off the road and into the river," Maggie said. "He is presumed dead."

"You'll forgive me if I don't shed a tear of remorse," Laura said.

"That's understandable," Maggie agreed. "But you should know that my husband is the former sheriff of Dogwood Mountain County. Brett Mission."

"I know Sheriff Mission," Laura said, smiling for the first time. "You're his wife?"

"Yes, and you know he's retired now, right?"

"I heard that." Laura nodded. "Anyway, I'm still confused about why you're here."

"Brett and Andrew worked together on this case about eighteen years ago," Ruby said. "Andrew showed up a few days ago out of the blue to talk to Brett about it."

"Not only did he want to speak with my husband about the case," Maggie said. "But he claimed he was receiving blackmail letters himself. He came to see if Brett was dealing with the same thing."

"Someone started sending the letters again?"

"According to Andrew, yes," Maggie said.

"We found your father's name in some of the notes from the original case," Ruby said.

"And you wanted to see what my father might remember about it," Laura said, nodding her head. "Unfortunately, he won't be telling you anything."

"We can see that," Maggie said. "We're sorry for bothering you."

"I don't understand something," Laura said before Maggie reached the door to Malcolm's room. "Why are you here? Why isn't your husband or another law enforcement officer here to ask questions?"

"Let's just say that the sudden appearance of Andrew Finley in my husband's life has complicated the investigation."

"An FBI agent visited us and asked questions about Brett," Ruby said. "Andrew Finley put Brett under the microscope of suspicion."

"They think your husband started this?" Laura asked Maggie.

"They're questioning him," Maggie said. "That's why I decided to take matters into my own hands."

"You've got some nerve," Laura said, smiling. "I like that. You don't want to wait around for them to figure things out."

"For the record," Maggie said. "Not only was all of this a shock to Brett, but he couldn't have had anything to do with it."

"It never crossed my mind that he did," Laura said. "Anyway, I'm afraid I can't help you much. The only thing I can tell you is that my father had rock solid alibis that proved he was not the one sending the letters."

"We read that too," Ruby said. "We just thought he might have remembered some details about it that would help us figure out what's going on now."

"I wish I could do more," Laura said. "I was a bit younger when all of this took place. My father moved down here shortly after the case went cold."

"Do you remember anything yourself?" Maggie asked. "I know that was a long time ago."

"I just remember how stressed out my father got." Laura rested her hip on the side of her father's chair again. "They rummaged through his office three separate times, then they tore apart his house looking for evidence. I remember something about a pen."

"A Germantown Rollerball," Ruby said.

"Yes, that's it," Laura said. "I think that's what they were looking for, evidence that my father had one. Only, my dad wouldn't have known a fancy pen from a dollar store disposable pen."

"Thanks for your time," Maggie said. "We're sorry we bothered you."

"One last thing," Laura said. "Is it true what you said about Andrew Finley? Is he really gone?"

"His vehicle went off the road and into the river," Ruby said simply.

They walked in silence back down the hall toward the stairwell. Maggie held the door for Ruby but said nothing as they made their way to the car. She backed out of the parking space and headed down the long driveway toward Sassafras Hollow Road.

"That was interesting," Ruby said at last.

"To say the least," Maggie said. "Although I don't think we learned much."

"We've learned that Sarah Houston and Malcolm Price were both haunted by this case."

"And neither one of them is able to tell us why," Maggie said as they drove back to the farm.

"I feel like this case just got bigger." Ruby sighed.

"You do? I thought we just eliminated two potential suspects. I guess we can talk more about it with the girls in a little while."

A short while later, they arrived at the house, happy to see Naomi and Myra were already there.

"Hey, you two," Myra said, emerging from the back porch.

"You could have gone inside." Ruby shook her head.

"I'm not going inside your house without you here," Naomi said.

"Let's all go inside now," Ruby said, directing them all to take a seat at the kitchen table. "I have some salmon dip in the refrigerator and some wine in the cooler."

"I can't wait any longer," Myra announced. "Why don't the two of you fill us in on what you learned this afternoon."

"Well, to start, it seems that Maggie and I have different perspectives on what we learned today," Ruby explained. "Maggie thinks we eliminated two suspects, but as far as I'm concerned, we just opened Pandora's box to an entirely new set of suspects." She opened the door to her large refrigerator and began pulling out trays of sliced cheese and salmon dip.

"Like whom?" Naomi asked.

"Members of Sarah Houston's family and Malcolm Price's family," Ruby said. "Both family members we met today described how Andrew Finley ruined their loved ones' lives and both of them certainly could have forced Andrew off the road."

"Do you mean because of the investigation?" Myra asked.

"That's exactly what I mean." Ruby moved to a small nook in the kitchen and opened the door to the wine fridge.

"But you don't agree with her?" Naomi asked Maggie.

"It isn't that I disagree, I just hadn't thought of it that way. But now, after hearing her explanation, I'm afraid I do agree."

"We have no idea who might have wanted to run Andrew off the road, do we?" Myra asked.

"No, we don't," Maggie said. "But that might not be a bad thing for Brett. There are so many potential suspects that the focus should be on those people and not on him."

"What do we do now?" Myra asked.

"Now we sit back and enjoy this good food and a glass of wine," Ruby answered, raising a glass.

"And tomorrow we look into Larry McVie," Maggie said.

CHAPTER NINE

"Where were you today?" Brett questioned Maggie when she walked in the house two hours later.

"I spent some time with Ruby and the other girls," Maggie said. It wasn't a lie, but she had no desire to describe her activities of the afternoon.

"I didn't hear from you for a while."

"I assumed it would be a good idea for the two of us to take a little break," Maggie said. She moved to the freezer and opened the door in search of something for dinner.

"Do you want to know how my day went?"

"I assume it went well, since you're still here."

"I had another visit from Agent Johnson," Brett said.

Maggie turned around immediately and faced him. She closed the freezer door behind her. "Agent Johnson was back?"

Brett took a seat at the table and nodded his head slowly. "She was, and she had some good news for me. She came to inform me that I've moved to the bottom of her suspect list. I'm not entirely off the hook, but she's looking in other directions."

"Okay," Maggie said. "Did she say who she's looking into?"

"No one I know personally," Brett said. Maggie exhaled slowly in relief. For a moment, she feared that she might be in the FBI agent's crosshairs.

"Is there any news on Andrew himself?"

"I just learned that they intend to pull his truck from the river this weekend." Brett grimaced. "Since they've been unable to recover his body, they're assuming he's still in the truck."

"Why so long?" Maggie asked.

"Because they have to wait until they have a big enough truck to pull it out of the river." Brett folded his hands under his chin. "A team is coming down from Kansas City to help out."

"That's good news, isn't it?"

"It absolutely is good news. Maybe now we'll get some more answers."

"We can only hope," Maggie agreed. "Anyway, what do you feel like for dinner?"

"What about lasagna?" Brett smiled. "Let's go out."

"Let me change my clothes." Maggie ran her hand down the front of her shirt.

"Is that what you wore to work?"

"Yes, I didn't get a chance to change."

"I thought you said you spent time with the girls this afternoon," Brett said.

"Right." Maggie nodded. "I didn't come home first."

"That's not like you," Brett said, eyeing her suspiciously. "Normally, you don't go anywhere without a shower."

"I guess today was an exception." Maggie rushed down the hallway toward her bedroom. She reached in her closet for a fresh set of clothes and headed to the bathroom where she took a fast shower.

"Feel better?" Brett asked when she emerged from the bathroom.

"I do," Maggie said. "Are we ready to go?"

"If you still want to go."

"Why wouldn't I want to go?" Maggie asked.

"I don't know," Brett said. "I thought maybe visiting Sarah Houston's sister or finding Malcolm Price in his assisted living facility might have been too taxing today."

"Who called while I was in the bathroom?" Maggie groaned.

"Brooks did," Brett said. "He wanted to make sure to let me know his office received a complaint from Laura Price about your visit to her father."

"Really? That's shocking to me."

"What part is the most shocking?" Brett asked. "The fact that I found out or the fact that Brooks told me?"

"Neither," Maggie said. "I thought we got on well with Laura."

"So, you're not upset that he told me?"

"Why would I be?" Maggie shrugged.

"Why didn't you tell me about it when you got home?"

"Let's stop this," Maggie said. "We both know this isn't going to end well."

"Stop what? Lying to each other?" Brett asked.

"First of all, I never lied to you. We need to stop answering questions with more questions. Let's get to the point. The girls and I got together and decided to look into things ourselves. I didn't tell you when you I got home because I didn't want to argue with you about it."

"Then you lied to me," Brett said. "You set this whole thing up so I wouldn't know what you were doing today."

"I didn't lie to you," Maggie said. "I made a decision based on our recent conversations. I planned to tell you about what happened later but chose not to do it the second I got home."

"Why are you trying so hard to excuse this?"

"I'm not trying hard to do anything," Maggie said. "I'm a grown woman who made a decision. I never intended to keep this from you forever, but I did decide to pick my battles when I came home. You can believe me or not, but right now, I'll be in the truck waiting for you to drive us to the Italian restaurant. I'm tired and I'm hungry."

"Maggie," Brett called after her as she walked out the back door.

Moments later, he pulled the door closed behind him and headed for the truck. He opened the driver's door and slid in behind the wheel without another word to his wife. They rode in silence to the Italian restaurant.

"Don't you dare get out of the truck," Brett said when he turned the truck off in the restaurant parking lot.

"What are you talking about?" Maggie asked as he shut the door. Before she could get her own door open, Brett appeared outside and opened it for her.

"Tonight, I'm going to open the door for my wife," Brett said. He offered his hand to her and helped her out of the truck. "And after the way we ended things at the house, I promise to be on my best behavior for dinner."

"Before we go in, I just want you to know that I intended to tell you about today. I just chose to wait."

"I'm not happy that you possibly put yourself in danger behind my back," Brett said. "Although I understand you and I know why you did it. I was wrong to accuse you of lying. I know it's just an excuse to say this, but I haven't felt like myself since Andrew came back to town."

"I think that's a legitimate feeling," Maggie said. "Let's just go inside and enjoy dinner. We can talk more about this later when we aren't hungry."

CHAPTER TEN

"How upset was he?" Myra asked the minute Maggie walked in the door of the donut shop the following morning.

She set her things in the office on the desk and returned to the kitchen for a clean apron. "Fairly upset, but things were good by the end of the night."

"I'm glad to hear it," Myra said. She headed to the front with Naomi to prepare the dining room for opening.

"Were things really okay between you and Brett?" Ruby asked when they were alone in the kitchen.

"Well, he wasn't too happy at first," Maggie admitted

"Myra told us Brooks called to chat about our visit to see Malcolm."

"His daughter had a complaint." Maggie nodded. "Which really shocked me, you know."

"Did he try to ban you from ever investigating again?"

Maggie frowned. "I told him I planned to fill him in on what happened, just not the second I walked through the door."

"Did he buy that?" Ruby asked.

"I wasn't just making it up. I'm not some teenage Nancy Drew wannabe or something, sneaking out of her parents' house at night."

"I didn't mean to offend you."

"You didn't. I just made up my mind that I was going to play this straight. I might not have told him where I was going to begin with, but I had no plans to hide it."

"Good on you, then." Ruby turned back to the prep table where she had just begun to lay out her fixings for the day's boxed lunches. "I suppose we ought to get busy with our real jobs."

"There is one more thing," Maggie said. She looked up and smiled as Myra and Naomi entered the kitchen through the swinging door.

"What's going on?" Naomi asked.

"I was about to tell Ruby what Brett told me last night," Maggie said. "Agent Johnson, the same woman who stopped by here, paid him a visit yesterday."

"Is that a good thing?" Myra asked. She took a seat on Orson's stool.

"Actually, it was. She stopped by to inform him that he's no longer at the top of her suspect list. He's comfortably at the very bottom."

"But he is still a suspect?" Ruby asked.

"Apparently so, but Brett took it as a good thing."

"So, then what's the plan today?" Naomi asked. "Are we still looking into Larry McVie?"

"I think that's a good idea," Maggie said. "By the way, Brett told me the vehicle Andrew was driving should be pulled from the river over the weekend. There is a crew headed down here from Kansas City with a large truck or whatever."

"Hopefully we have a better idea of what happened to Finley when they pull it out," Ruby said.

Maggie headed to the storage room and began collecting ingredients for the cinnamon rolls. She brought a tray of croissant dough out next and began working on the cronuts for the display case. Ruby and the others worked diligently at their normal stations. After nine, Orson wandered into the kitchen and took his usual spot on his stool.

Once the display case was adequately filled, Maggie informed Ruby that it was time for their morning break. Ruby agreed to meet her at the booth on the side of the front counter with a snack. Maggie filled two coffee mugs and took her seat.

Before Ruby could join her, Maggie was surprised when her cell phone rang, and Brett's number appeared on the screen. "Honey," she said when she answered. "Is everything okay?"

"Yeah, I suppose so," Brett said. "I just wanted to let you know that I found out from the county that the crew from Kansas City is already here."

"What does that mean?" Maggie asked.

"It means that the process to extract Andrew's truck from the river is underway now. I just wanted to let you know before you begin any of your extra-curricular activities this afternoon."

"What was that all about?" Ruby asked when she took her seat across from Maggie just as their phone call ended.

"They're already pulling Andrew's truck out of the river."

"Right now?" Ruby asked. She stirred her creamer into her coffee. "What happened?"

"I guess there was an opening in their schedule, and they decided to head down earlier than expected." Maggie shrugged. "I'm going to take it as a good thing."

"Are we still up for a field trip this afternoon?" Ruby asked.

"Absolutely."

Maggie returned to the kitchen after her break with Ruby. The rest of the day moved by swiftly. Myra and Naomi had the bulk of the cleaning done less than thirty minutes after closing time. Maggie retreated into the office and began searching through the notes. She took her seat in the office chair and scanned each of the pages for information.

Her phone rang again. She picked it up immediately when she spotted Brett's number on the screen again.

"What's going on?" she asked.

"They pulled it out, Maggie," Brett said. "He wasn't there."

"Is he in the river then?"

"When they pulled the truck out of the bottom of the river, it was completely intact. In fact, they found several letters wrapped up in a bag inside the glove box."

"He kept the letters he got in the glove box of his truck?" Maggie asked.

"That's what I was told," Brett said. "But I'll admit I'm a little confused."

"Tell me one thing. Do they assume that Andrew Finley is still alive?"

"I'm not sure, Maggie," Brett said. "Right now, I'm not sure what to think."

CHAPTER ELEVEN

"What do you think this means?" Ruby asked Maggie. They were parked together at the entrance of a small community a few miles south of Hunter Springs. Maggie had produced the address for Larry McVie, cousin to one of the blackmail letter victims.

"I don't think it's clear that Andrew was killed when his truck went into the river," Maggie said.

"I don't think so either," Ruby said.

"As a matter of fact, I have a strange feeling about this. I don't know what to think just yet," Maggie said.

"Well, maybe after we talk to Larry, things will be a little clearer," Ruby suggested. "Do you know which one is his?" She pointed to the row of townhomes connected on the other side of the entrance. They had agreed to leave their vehicles parked outside of the community. According to the signage in the front, only permitted vehicles were allowed into the neighborhood.

"I think his is the third from the end," Maggie said, pointing to the first set of townhomes. "Let's just walk up to his front door and see what he has to say."

"I think I would prefer it if my truck was just a few feet away instead of half a block," Ruby said. She reluctantly fell in step next to Maggie.

They continued down the sidewalk until they reached another walkway that led to the front of the building. Maggie hastened her step as they approached Larry McVie's front door. She intended to go through with it, but in her heart, she felt like it was a moot point, just another part of the investigation to check off her list. Her instinct told her they were looking in the wrong place.

Maggie raised her hand and knocked firmly on the door. They could hear rustling on the other side and moment later, the door opened. A disheveled man

IT CURD BE MURDER

stood on the other side. "Yeah, what is it?" he demanded.

"Are you Larry McVie?" Ruby asked. "Hugh's cousin?"

"My cousin died a long time ago," Larry said. "Who's asking?"

"Just a couple of people looking into an old case," Maggie said. "Do you remember much about it?"

"Go away," Larry said. He began to close the door.

"Are we familiar to you?" Maggie asked suddenly. Ruby questioned her with a look.

"I don't know you," Larry said. He leaned slightly against the front door. "I don't know your voice."

"Can you see us?" Ruby asked, catching on.

"I ain't seen nothing for more than fifteen years," Larry snapped. "That's what the diabetes did to me. Now what do you want?"

"Do you remember Andrew Finley, the man from up north who helped investigate your cousin's death?" Maggie asked quickly. "My husband worked with him on that case. He showed up here less than a week ago claiming the letters had started again."

"And we just wanted to check with you and see if you had heard or seen anything," Ruby finished.

"No, ma'am," Larry said, shaking his head. "Not that I could see any threatening letters if they were sent to me anyway."

"Has anyone been around to ask you any questions?" Maggie asked.

"Nary a soul," Larry said. "I don't want anything to do with this anymore. I lost someone I loved."

"Okay, then," Maggie said. "We're sorry for bothering you."

"Yeah, thank you for your time," Ruby said. They turned from the door just as Larry slammed it shut behind them. Maggie said nothing as they made their way back down the sidewalk to the front entrance of the community.

"What is it?" Maggie mused. "I know you're bursting to ask me a question."

"I'm just surprised. You didn't push him very hard."

"He's blind, and I'm sure he wasn't faking it. How much could he have had to do with this?"

"Okay, but there was something else I found rather peculiar."

"I wonder if it's the same thing I'm thinking about," Maggie said.

"Of all the people involved with the case eighteen years ago, Larry would be the first person I would question if I were Andrew."

"That's the same thing I was thinking," Maggie said. "He would be the easiest person to talk to."

"Right, because Sarah Houston is already dead, and Malcolm Price is too far gone. So, why didn't Andrew seek these people out, too?" Ruby asked. "From the moment he stepped into the donut shop asking about Brett until we met for dinner later that night, he would have had plenty of time to further his investigation, but he didn't seem to question anyone."

"Exactly my thoughts," Maggie said. "I think there's something else going on here. There's been something else going on this entire time."

"Where are you going now?" Ruby asked when Maggie opened her car door.

"I have one more stop I want to make."

"Did you find someone else to talk to?"

"No." Maggie shook her head. "I'm going to see Gretchen again. I know Andrew wasn't there long, but maybe she can think of something she noticed about him that might help us."

"Just promise me you aren't going to get yourself in trouble."

"I'm not going to get myself in trouble." Maggie chuckled.

"I'll see you at my house in a little while." She climbed into the cab of her pickup and waved.

Maggie picked up her phone before she pulled away from the entrance. She checked her messages and decided to call Brett after her visit to the Dogwood House.

"Gretchen is inside," Albert announced to her when she pulled into the driveway. He nodded toward the large house that had once belonged to her aunt.

"There's just that same single guest here today, but she keeps to herself. Feel free to head in."

"Albert," Maggie said as she stepped out of her car. "What did you think of Andrew Finley?"

"He was strange."

"How so?" Maggie asked. "Did he say something odd to you?"

He shook his head. "No, but he was supposed to be here for a while. I thought it was odd that the only thing he had with him was a briefcase."

"He didn't carry any luggage with him?"

"Nothing," Albert said.

"Thank you." Maggie knocked on the back door and let herself inside.

"What a nice surprise." Gretchen smiled when Maggie walked into the kitchen.

"I'm not sure if you've heard, but Andrew's vehicle was pulled out of the river a little while ago."

Her smile quickly turned to a frown. "No, I hadn't heard that."

"The thing is," Maggie said slowly. "Andrew Finley's body wasn't in his vehicle."

"No kidding," Gretchen breathed. "What are they saying?"

"They haven't said anything yet," Maggie said. "Anyway, that's why I'm here. They found some of the threatening letters in Andrew's truck. I wondered if it would be okay if I looked over his room."

"You're welcome to look," Gretchen said. "But I did clean the room already."

"I have no doubt it's clean," Maggie said. "I want to take a look for myself."

"Go ahead and look around in the small bedroom. You know your way around, just be aware that I do have a guest in the main bedroom."

Maggie nodded and headed down the long hallway to the first guest room. Maggie pushed the door open and turned on the light. A single full-size bed was arranged next to the window. She studied the items on top of the tall wooden dresser just inside the door, then moved to the small desk that was set against the wall next to the bed.

Gretchen was right. The room had been thoroughly untouched. Maggie hesitated in front of the small desk. She reached for the top drawer and studied the contents. She pushed the drawer back in and headed to the closet. When she opened the closet door, all she found were the neatly folded linens on the shelf inside. Several empty hangers hung on a rod, but there was nothing on the floor, nothing to find at all.

Maggie dropped her arms and shook her head. Perhaps she had made a mistake in coming. There was nothing to find. Her eyes moved to the side of the bed. A small, braided rug had been placed on the floor, giving guests a warmer surface to step on when they first wake up in the morning. Unlike the other items in the room, the rug seemed slightly off center. Maggie gripped the footboard and lowered herself to the floor. With the help of her cell phone flashlight, she searched under the bed, but came up with nothing.

"What are you doing?" a voice came from behind her. "What are you doing in this room?"

She raised herself up with the help of the end of the bed and turned to face the woman. "Oh, hello. My name is Maggie."

"Are you staying in this room now?"

Maggie eyed the woman carefully. "I'm not. I'm actually a friend of the man who was staying here recently. Do you know him?"

She already knew the answer, but suddenly it seemed like the right question to ask.

"Not well, but I did meet him. We were supposed to go on a date." She glared at Maggie. "Are you his wife or something?"

Maggie cleared her throat. "I'm not his wife, but I'm afraid I don't have good news about Andrew." She began to explain things very vaguely to the woman, just to see her reaction.

"Isn't this just the icing on the cake?" The woman sat down on the edge of the bed. "I finally think I meet a nice guy and I find out this."

Maggie sat down next to her. "What's your name?"

"Elaine."

"What can you tell me about Andrew? What sort of things did you talk about?"

Elaine looked at Maggie and hung her head. "Well, as you know he's a very attractive man. He was nice to me and told me he was going to take me out and show me his house in the area. He said it was huge, and since I work in interior design, he said he'd interview me for the job of decorating it. We had the arts in common. He was a writer and I worked in design. We even discussed the possibility of working together on a project."

"Wow, that sounds like it would have been a good opportunity," Maggie said, concerned that Andrew had told Elaine he lived in the area. This information, combined with what Albert had said about him arriving with just a briefcase, seemed odd.

Elaine nodded. "I can't believe he just took off like that, and now it sounds like he's dead. I seriously have the worst luck."

"I'm sure you're great at your job and will find plenty of clients. In fact, if you live in the area, perhaps you can show me some of your work, and I can recommend you to people that may be in need."

"Really? Gee, that would be great. I live about two hours from here, and I'm pretty down on my luck. I really thought I'd met a great catch. I came here to clear my head, but maybe this trip won't turn out to be so bad after all."

"I'd be happy to. Do you have a portfolio or anything with you?"

Elaine nodded eagerly and jumped up from the bed. "Stay right here, I'll be back!"

Maggie felt bad for the woman. Elaine had only known Andrew for a few hours and seemed to have gotten a bit too attached, much too fast.

"Here we are," Elaine said, just a moment later. She laid out a large folder of photographs on the bed between them. "This one is from the very first house I worked on. I like to show it first so I can clearly point out the progression from then," she turned the page, "until now."

When the page turned, Maggie's face fell, and her heart began to pound. "What's this?"

"Oh, this is the most recent home I did. The client was amazing to work with and the budget was…"

"No." Maggie pointed at the pen that had rolled to her leg. "What is that?"

The woman reached across the folder and picked it up. "Oh, funnily enough that belonged to your friend,

Andrew. He let me use it to sign Gretchen's guestbook. He told me to keep it."

Maggie looked around the room and ripped a tissue from the box next to the bed. She carefully took the pen from Elaine's fingers and read the inscription again, even though she knew very well what she had seen the first time.

CHAPTER TWELVE

"I need to see you," Maggie said to Brett as she stood outside of the bed and breakfast.

"Where are you?"

"At the Dogwood House. Get here as fast as you can."

"Maggie, I'm not alone," Brett said. "Agent Johnson is with me."

"Perfect. Bring her with you."

Ten minutes later, Brett pulled up in his pickup and a dark colored sedan parked on the road in front. Maggie leaned against the side of her car and waited, her mind reeling.

"What's going on here, Mrs. Mission?" the agent asked as she approached.

Maggie said nothing in response but held up the pen.

"What is that?" Brett asked.

"It's a pen Elaine Archer was given by Andrew Finley."

"Okay, what is it about this situation that requires a visit from me?" Agent Johnson asked.

"Elaine is a guest here at the bed and breakfast and she believed that her and Andrew had become fast friends. He not only asked her out on a date, but he also offered to interview her for the job of doing the décor for his house in the area."

"I'm sorry, what?" Brett asked, his eyes narrowing.

"What is so significant about this to you?" Agent Johnson asked at the same time.

"Maggie, is that what I think it is?" Brett asked. He stepped closer to the pen and examined it without touching it.

"It appears to be. Elaine said Andrew let her use it to sign Gretchen's guest book and then he told her to keep it," Maggie said.

"I can't believe it," Brett said, still staring at the pen. "She said he told her he has a house around here?"

"Can the two of you stop for a minute?" Agent Johnson took a closer look at the pen. Her eyes lit up and her face finally registered understanding. "Stay right there," she said, then turned and ran back down the driveway toward her vehicle. A second later, she popped the lid to her trunk and began rummaging through a box in the back. She slammed the lid shut and walked back toward them, holding a plastic bag in her hand. "Why don't you just drop that right inside this bag for me?"

Maggie dropped it inside and looked to Brett. "That's what she said. I don't think she's lying about anything."

"I'll go find out," Agent Johnson said. She marched to the front door of the Dogwood House.

"She should find out if Elaine knows where his house is too," Brett said, watching as the agent ran off.

Maggie grinned. "I already asked. She said that he told her that it was the biggest house on Branch Street. Branch Street… you know, behind the river."

He shook his head. "This is insane."

"Brett, do you think it's possible that Andrew is alive and he's hiding out there?"

He was silent for a moment then let out a heavy sigh. "I don't understand why, but I do think it's possible. In fact, the discovery of the pen basically proves he was the one behind the blackmail letters. Do you think it was him all along?" Brett asked, a grim look coming over his face.

Maggie held up her hands in front of her. "I don't know enough to say that he was the one who started it nearly twenty years ago, but I'm quite sure he was up to something. You said there were letters found in his truck when it was pulled from the river, right?"

"Right, but I was told that none of the envelopes had addresses on them," Brett said. He stopped for a moment and gazed at his wife. "Oh. None of the envelopes were addressed."

"I have to go," he announced suddenly. "I need to talk to Agent Johnson. She needs to be on Branch Street, not here."

CHAPTER THIRTEEN

"I think it's funny," Orson declared later that week.

"What's funny?" Brooks asked. They were seated in their usual spots around the bonfire at Ruby's farm.

"I think it's funny that I was right again. It's getting to be rather absurd that one man can be so right, so often."

Maggie cackled. "Oh, dear. Orson, you really are something else. What was it that you were right about this time?"

"Well, I very clearly remember saying that love and romance make people do crazy things. It clouds people's good sense. That's why Andrew let that woman keep his pen. He may have never gotten caught if it wasn't for that."

"I suppose he was right about that," Myra agreed. "Although, I think us girls should take a little credit for what we accomplished, too."

"So do I," Naomi chimed in. "We were helpful too."

"I'm just glad that we were able to work together and eventually get things figured out. I just hated that Brett's name was even part of this," Ruby said.

"I am, too," Maggie said. "I couldn't have done this alone. Thanks, girls."

"Hey, what about me?" Brett asked

"What about you?" Maggie teased. "If I remember correctly, you were against my involvement from the beginning."

"What did Finley have to say when you arrested him?" Brooks asked, interrupting the conversation.

"Unfortunately, I didn't arrest him." Brett laughed. "But I was there when Agent Johnson put the handcuffs on him."

"Did he resist?" Myra asked.

"He didn't get the chance." Brett puffed out his chest. "By the time he knew we were there, twenty cops had surrounded his place."

"Exactly where was his place, anyway?" Ruby asked.

"It was a large home along the river," Brett answered.

Brooks shook his head. "Not far from where his truck went in, I assume."

"Within walking distance. He plunged his truck into the river and stood on the bank until he couldn't see any more oncoming traffic, then simply walked to his house," Brett explained.

"But why?" Orson spoke up. "What reason did he have to come here and claim that he was a victim of this blackmail letter scheme after all of these years? Why did he do this?"

Brett leaned forward and warmed his hands over the fire. "First, Agent Johnson figured out that it was him all along. He started this whole thing to cover up some wrongdoings in the sheriff's office twenty years ago. You see, Andrew Finley was a consultant, but he was also a bit of a fixer back in the day."

"It turns out the department was under investigation when the first letter appeared," Maggie added.

"Yeah, and the attention suddenly turned away from the issues at the department when the letters started," Brett said. "Agent Johnson learned that, all these years later, he was trying to cash in on the case."

"How would he do that?" Naomi asked.

Ruby gasped. "I know! Can I say it?"

The group all turned to her with confused looks on their faces.

She continued, "I think I know why he came back and started things up again."

"Go for it," Orson said. "Tell the rest of the class."

"Andrew would have had extensive notes about this case over the years. Especially if he was the one doing it because he would have been trying hard to make it look real. He was going to write a book about it, wasn't he?" Ruby asked, standing from her seat. "The reemergence of the case would benefit book sales."

Maggie beamed and stood to hug her best friend. "She has a writer brain, folks."

"I'm right?" Ruby asked. "He told me that night at dinner that he was a writer, and all I kept thinking about during this whole thing was how interesting it would be as a book. I might write non-fiction, but I still love a good story."

"You are right," Maggie said, squeezing her harder.

"No wonder he balked against the thought of you taking this to the cold case group," Brooks added. "He couldn't risk them seeing through his charade."

"I'm so proud of all of you," Maggie said. "None of this would have been possible without you guys."

"Don't sell yourself short," Orson said. "You're no slouch at this yourself."

"Thanks." Maggie walked over to him and put her hands on his shoulders.

"Yeah, thanks, Orson," Brett agreed.

"For what?" Orson asked.

"For saying what I should have been saying all along. My wife is a force to be reckoned with when she sets her mind to something."

AUTHOR'S NOTE

I'd love to hear your thoughts on my books, the storylines, and anything else that you'd like to comment on—reader feedback is very important to me. My contact information, along with some other helpful links, is listed on the next page. If you'd like to be on my list of "folks to contact" with updates, release and sales notifications, etc.… just shoot me an email and let me know. Thanks for reading!

Also…

… if you're looking for more great reads, Summer Prescott Books publishes several popular series by outstanding Cozy Mystery authors.

CONTACT SUMMER PRESCOTT BOOKS PUBLISHING

Blog and Book Catalog: http://summerprescottbooks.com

Email: summer.prescott.cozies@gmail.com

And…be sure to check out the Summer Prescott Cozy Mysteries fan page and Summer Prescott Books Publishing Page on Facebook – let's be friends!

To sign up for our fun and exciting newsletter, which will give you opportunities to win prizes and swag, enter contests, and be the first to know about New Releases, click here: http://summerprescottbooks.com